Kameesha

Other Titles from Word out Books

- The Wisconsin Prison Cookbook by Eric Hainstock
- Poems of a Captured Soul by Fabion D. Brown
- Stonyford Submission by Bennie Ray Murdock
- Stonyford Submission II by Bennie Ray Murdock
- Stonyford Submission III by Bennie Ray Murdock
- Rocket Cat: Battle of the Bands by Keven A. Miles
- The Incredible Adventures of Jeffy the Squirrel: Jeffy Goes to Hollywood by Keven A. Miles
- The Incredible Adventures of Jeffy the Squirrel: Jeffy Goes to Space
- The Incredible Adventures of Jeffy the Squirrel: Uncle Sammy Comes to Visit

Visit our website for a full list of titles from our imprints at:

www.az-entertainmentllc.com/order

Kameesha

Ronnie Redd Rice

Wagoner Oklahoma

Published by Word Out Books An imprint of AZ Entertainment Group LLC

cover design by AZ Designs

ISBN: 978-1-947035-69-0

For inquiries, including bulk orders of 100 or more, please contact:
AZ Entertainment Group LLC
PO BOX 854
Wagoner, OK 74477-0854

Email: info@az-entertainmentllc.com
Website: www.az-entertainmentllc.com

Printed in the United States of America

Dedicated to Ms. Tracy Powell
one of a kind

CHAPTER 1

Darren was getting a little upset. What was supposed to be a three-hour drive had turned into a slow, cautious crawl. Snow continued to fall along the highway, more like a constant mist than a storm. It barely covered the road, but traffic moved at a cautious pace. Nobody wanted to risk a collision. Even the truck drivers were being extra attentive.

Darren had just passed Jackson, Michigan. He grabbed his phone and called his girl, Kim. When she answered, he put her on speaker.

"Are you here yet, bae?"

"Not yet, Kim. I should be about thirty more minutes."

"Hurry up! I want to see your face."

"The highway's moving, but I'm doing my best."

"You want me safe, don't you?"

"Yeah! It's been weeks since the last time I saw you."

"I miss you too, Kim. Let me get back to concentrating on the highway. I'll call you as soon as I pull up at the apartment complex."

"Okay," Kim said. "I love you."

"Love you too." Darren was all smiles as the call ended.

As he looked at the sign, he saw he was one mile away from his exit: Taylor, Michigan. Darren felt a wave of relief as he made the turn off the highway. He continued driving down Telegraph Road, passing a few red lights. Two left turns later, Darren pulled up to the apartment complex. It was about one-thirty in the morning.

Darren stepped out of the car and grabbed his overnight bag. The cold winter air hit his face, and he began to walk a little faster. He reached into his pocket, grabbed his phone, and called Kim.

"Hello!"

"Come and unlock the door."

"Okay."

Kim rushed downstairs to open the door for her boo. She was all smiles when she opened the door for Darren. Kim embraced Darren so tightly he could barely get inside the apartment.

"Kim, sweetheart, it's cold outside. Can I get inside first?"

Kim wasn't trying to hear what Darren was saying. She missed her man, and for a brief moment, Kim was happy.

Darren continued to struggle to get inside the apartment. After convincing Kim to ease her grip from around his waist, he was finally able to close the door. Feeling the heat inside, Darren continued to hold Kim as he looked around. There were baby toys lying around and a playpen in the corner.

Darren caressed Kim's stomach. "Is there something you want to tell me?"

Kim quickly caught on to what Darren was doing. "Nobody is pregnant, Darren. Those are my sister's things. Sometimes I babysit my niece while she goes to work."

"Is she here now?"

"No. She knew you were coming into town and knew that I needed this weekend for us."

Darren gave a big kiss on Kim's forehead. "Thank you for that, bae."

"You're welcome."

"I need to take a piss real quick. I didn't pull over at any time.

I was trying to get here and out of that snow. I'll be right back."

As Darren headed upstairs to the bathroom, Kim drifted into heavy thoughts. Would Darren be a good father? Their relationship had been good so far. They had been seeing each other for the last nine months. The long distance didn't really bother her. They talked on the phone every day, and Darren drove up every few weeks.

At some point, Kim wanted to ask Darren what his thoughts were about them being together full-time.

Kim's focus was interrupted when she heard the toilet flush.

"Ahhh... I feel a lot lighter. How about you come upstairs and give me a back rub?" Darren said.

"How about I give you a kiss on the lips and let me get my beauty sleep?" Kim said.

"I'm not tired," Darren said. "I just want to relax and look at you."

"Darren, it's almost three in the morning. Everybody in Michigan is asleep."

"Not true. Stop looking at me from the bottom of the stairs and come up," Darren said.

Kim turned off the light downstairs and headed up the stairs.

*

Demisha continued to cry as she blew her nose. She had been calling her potential baby's father for the last hour. It was going on three o'clock in the morning. Her mother was in the back room sleeping. She tried to be as quiet as she could, even as she hollered when the voicemail kept picking up.

"I need you to call me back. You're the only person that I slept with." Tears continued to fall from her face as she dialed the number one more time. The phone didn't even ring. It went straight to voicemail.

Refusing to lie down and go to sleep, She dialed her brother's number.

CHAPTER 2

Darren had just kicked off his all-black Air Forces and lay down on Kim's soft queen bed. It felt good to be off the road and finally relax his body. He had the whole weekend to chill with Kim.

Darren had planned the trip weeks in advance. He put in a request with his manager, Ky, at the Nike shoe factory. Ky was an older man, about fifty-five. He was stubborn and believed in hard work.

Darren had been working there since he was sixteen. The factory sat in a small shopping center in Gary, Indiana, on Grant Street, where everybody used to go hang out. But with low-income families struggling and unemployment steadily rising, most of the smaller stores had closed.

Darren was a people person when it came to shoes. He tried to match each pair with the customer's personality. In the hood, every growing teenager wanted to play basketball. Every pair of high-top Nikes and Converse was easy to sell. Darren needed some time off from work. Being a top shoe salesman was hard work.

Before Darren left, Ky told him to be back on Monday.

Darren quickly returned his attention to Kim, who was now crawling slowly across the bed toward him. He was captivated by her beauty, her caramel complexion and her 5'6" frame. Kim had her hair tied in a green scarf and wore green cotton pajamas to match.

"I've never seen somebody look this good going to sleep." Darren noticed a little makeup and eyeliner on her face.

"I always look this good when the queen goes to sleep," Kim said.

Darren pulled Kim close to his chest and held her tight. These were the days he missed, going home to nobody there to hug him.

Kim felt the loneliness too. She wanted Darren by her side at all times. The long distance was hard, but the subject of moving in together had never come up.

Just as Darren and Kim began getting intimate with a few kisses on the lips, Darren's phone started ringing. He pulled it out of his pocket and answered.

"Hello? Slow down—what's wrong?"

Demisha was all mumbles.

"Calm down and breathe, sis." Darren looked at Kim and passed the phone to her. "My sister asked to speak with you."

Kim looked confused and pressed the phone to her chest. She knew of Darren's sister but had never had a real conversation with her. "What do I say?" Kim asked, looking at Darren.

"Just see what's wrong. She won't stop crying. As her brother, I'm concerned."

Kim understood the love Darren had for his sister. She put the phone up to her ear. "This is Kim."

Kim's main focus was to listen as Darren stood there with a puzzled look on his face. What could his sister want to say to his girlfriend instead of him? After about ten minutes on the phone, Kim ended the call.

"Wait!" Darren said. "Why you hang up?"

"She didn't want to talk anymore. Your sister said she was tired and was going to try to get some sleep."

"What did she say, Kim?"

"Slow down, bae. I'm still trying to process how to tell you."

"Did something happen to our momma?"

"No."

"Did Ky call looking for me?"

"No. Why would he call your sister looking for you?"

"You got five seconds to tell me."

"What's the rush?"

"It's almost four in the morning, and my sister is calling, crying. That's the rush."

"Okay," Kim said. "I get it. First, it's a woman thing. And as her brother, she didn't want to tell you and have you start yelling at her. Your sister is pregnant."

Darren jumped off the bed and began grabbing his shoes.

"Where you going, Darren?"

"Getting back on the highway."

"Don't be stupid. It's cold outside, and you need to get some sleep."

"Right now my adrenaline is pumping, and I'll sleep once I make it back home."

"Don't be ridiculous. Just relax, and let's talk about it."

"Kim, what's there to talk about? She ain't keepin' it."

Kim felt numb at the words Darren had just said. How could this day turn out so cold and hurtful? Kim sat back on the bed, completely silent.

Darren realized what he had said. He apologized for the comment. "I love kids, but my baby sister is a week shy of her seventeenth birthday, and she's pregnant."

Darren grabbed his little black bag and proceeded out of the bedroom and down the stairs. Once he got to the door, he noticed Kim wasn't behind him. Confused about what to do, Darren stood there. He was hurt inside and didn't know how to express his anger. Out of frustration, he began scratching his head, then headed back upstairs to talk to Kim.

"Me?"

"Did you call looking for me?"

"No. Why would he call your sister looking for you?"

"You and Eve seem to [illegible]."

"What are they [illegible]?"

"It's almost four in the morning, and my sister is calling, crying. That's the deal."

"Okay," Kim said. "I get it. First, it's a woman thing, and as a mother, [illegible] your [illegible] as you start [illegible] after your sister's pregnant."

[illegible] jumped up out of bed and began grabbing his shoes.

"Where are you going, Darren?"

"Getting [illegible] to the [illegible]."

"Don't be stupid. It's cold outside, and you need to get some sleep."

"Right now my adrenaline is pumping, and I'll sleep after I [illegible] make it back home."

"Don't be stupid. Just relax, and let's talk about it."

"Kim, what's there to talk about? She ain't [illegible] it."

Kim looked at the words Darren had just said [illegible] tried to turn on a [illegible] and [illegible] Kim sat back on the bed, completely silent.

Darren realized what he had said. He apologized for the comment. "Honestly, this is crazy [illegible] week [illegible] of [illegible] Queen's birthday, and she's pregnant."

Darren grabbed his little blue [illegible] and proceeded out of the bedroom and down the stairs. Once he got to the door, he noticed Kim wasn't behind him. Confused about what to do, Darren stood there. He was [illegible] and didn't know how to express his anger. Out of frustration, he began scratching his head, then headed back upstairs to talk to Kim.

CHAPTER 3

Kim could no longer pretend she was sleeping as she continued to hear Darren snoring. She had barely gotten any sleep after the argument between them. Usually, Kim would have her legs wrapped around Darren, rubbing his goatee as they lay in bed, looking into each other's eyes. This Saturday morning felt different. There was no smile on her face.

She walked into the bathroom and took a hot shower. Once she got out, she did her hair and makeup, then stepped out feeling a little refreshed. She gave a quick glance at Darren, who was sleeping like nothing was wrong. Kim wanted to shake him so badly, just to wake him up out of spite. After deciding against it, she headed downstairs to cook breakfast. Maybe a little bacon and eggs would ease the tension. Darren had never complained about her cooking.

As Kim grabbed a non-stick skillet, she could hear Darren's heavy footsteps walking toward the bathroom.

*

Darren's eyes opened once Kim walked downstairs. He got up, stretched, and grabbed his phone. He immediately dialed his sister's number.

Same result. Voicemail. He went back upstairs, thinking

about how to undo his outburst with Kim. The mascara on her face had been messed up from the tears. Darren was weak in the knees when it came to Kim. He loved her very much. Any problems they had, they could usually work through and keep moving forward.

Darren had told Kim he was sorry, that any woman had the right to choose whether or not to have a baby. It was their body. He kept assuring her he wasn't leaving, that he wasn't upset anymore, and that they could talk in the morning. But once they got ready for bed, the separation was real.

Kim turned off the lamp and curled up in a ball on the left side of the bed. Darren followed suit, staring at the wall until his eyes got heavy.

Now, Darren could smell the bacon coming from downstairs. He was getting hungry. For a moment, he wondered if Kim had snuck downstairs to use the phone, to call her sister and tell her all their business, to get another woman's opinion.

Darren started washing his face and brushing his teeth. He didn't have a clue how today would play out, but he hoped to make the best of it. It would be another two or three weeks before he saw Kim again. Once he finished in the bathroom, he put on a fresh black tee and some gray sweats, then headed downstairs.

Kim was adding cheese to the scrambled eggs as she heard Darren coming down the stairs and walking into the small kitchen. There was a square wooden table with two chairs.

As Darren sat down, Kim kept her attention on the eggs. After a few more seconds, she grabbed a plate from the cabinet and put a heavy scoop of cheesy eggs on it. The bacon had drained some of the grease onto paper towels. Kim grabbed four slices of maple bacon and walked them over to Darren.

Darren had a big smile on his face. "Thank you."

Kim didn't say anything. She set the plate down and walked back to the stove to fix her own.

Darren could feel the heat in the kitchen.

After Kim sat down with her plate, Darren bowed his head and said a prayer over his food. Once he said amen, he grabbed his fork and went straight to the cheesy eggs. "Mmm. The eggs are scrumptious, bae. Thanks for cooking."

Kim ate slowly, looking around.

"Good morning. It's good to be thankful," Darren said. "I said good morning."

"Good morning," Kim replied.

Darren didn't like the nonchalant way she said it.

"Today is Saturday. How about we make the best of it? I don't want to argue or be mad once I get back on the highway to go home."

"So you just going to eat my food and leave?"

Kim stood up, about to storm out of the kitchen.

Darren grabbed her hand. "Wait."

He stood up and held her close. "Hear me out. I don't want you to feel any different toward me. I feel stupid for letting certain things come out of my mouth. Demisha is my kid sister, and I love her. If she decides to keep the baby, then I'll be the best uncle to her. And I want you by my side.

"You're a strong Black woman, and you've been independent since you were seventeen. Our relationship has many layers. If we keep peeling them back one by one, everything isn't going to be perfect. The communication between us has to be honest. I love you." Darren planted a kiss on Kim's cheek.

Kim started crying. "That's all I wanted to hear."

"How about you finish those eggs, and let's see what you can buy me?" Darren started laughing. "I only brought hundreds on me."

"You funny," Kim said.

As they continued eating their breakfast, Darren grabbed Kim's hand and squeezed it tight. Kim adored Darren's affection as she embraced the love she had for her man.

After Kim sat down with her plate, Darren bowed his head and said a prayer over his food. Once he said amen, he grabbed his fork and went straight to the cheesy eggs. "Mmm. The eggs are scrumptious, babe. Thanks for cooking."

Kim ate slowly, looking around.

"Good morning. It's good to be thankful," Darren said. "I said good morning."

"Good morning," Kim replied.

Darren didn't like the nonchalant way she spoke.

"Today is Saturday. Let's just make the best of it. I don't want to argue or be angry once I get back. I have a long way to go [illegible]."

"So you planning to eat my food and leave?"

Kim stood up as if to storm out of the kitchen.

Darren grabbed her hand. "Wait."

He stood up and held her close. "Hear me out. I don't want you to feel any different toward me. I'm sorry for letting certain things come out of my mouth. Dolphia is my kid sister, and I love her. If she decides to keep the baby, then I'll be the best uncle to her. And I want you by my side.

"You're a strong Black woman, and you've been my partner since you were seventeen. Our relationship has many layers. If we keep peeling them back one by one, everything isn't going to be perfect. The communication between us has to be honest. I love you," Darren placed a kiss on Kim's cheek.

Kim started crying. "That's all I wanted to hear."

"How about you finish those eggs, and let's see what you can buy me," Darren started laughing. "I only brought hundreds on me."

"You funny," Kim said.

As they continued eating their breakfast, Darren grabbed Kim's hand and squeezed it tight. Kim adored Darren's affection as she embraced the love she had for her man.

CHAPTER 4

Demisha continued to peep through the blinds across the street. Her baby's father, Keith, always showed up on Saturdays to hang out with his cousin Mark. Keith lived in Chicago with his mother, and every weekend he pulled up in her gray Astrovan.

Demisha and her best friend Cookie would intentionally be outside playing jump rope while the boys played catch in the street. They were always hitting the neighbors' cars with the football. Demisha was surprised nobody's window ever got busted.

Keith thought he was a good quarterback, always trying to show off his arm strength. He made sure Demisha was paying attention.

After a few weeks, Mark came across the street and talked to Demisha. Mark went to school with her brother Darren, and they used to hang out before Darren got a job and started driving out of town to see his girlfriend. So Demisha started communicating with Mark.

Mark was really dark with big teeth. When he talked, his teeth showed, and Demisha would laugh on the inside. He could be funny at times, but he was all business when Demisha was around.

"You know my cousin Keith thinks you're attractive," Mark said. "He said you're very noticeable. Why you and your friend Cookie always playing jump rope every Saturday?"

"It's something we like to do," Demisha said, keeping a

straight face, not wanting to show interest. "Why your cousin always think he Superman with the football? He can't run that fast, and instead of throwing the ball into your hands, he overthrows it and dents the cars parked on the curb."

"You got jokes! I'm gonna tell him you said all that when he show up."

"It's a question of when. Tell him to throw the football to me."

Mark said he would and walked back across the street.

Demisha rushed into the house and made sure her hair looked nice for when Keith arrived.

Hours later, Keith pulled up at Mark's house. It was around seven-thirty in the evening when Demisha noticed the van. She applied some styling gel to her hair and combed her afro back into one big ponytail. Then she put on denim blue shorts and a white halter top.

Darren would be home late, and her mother always had girl night in the kitchen with a few of her coworkers from the hospital: screaming, laughing, playing cards, smoking cigarettes, drinking, fussing about how all Black men cheat and why they refuse to walk away from their relationships.

Demisha knew her mother would be occupied all night, so she could spend extra time outside kicking it with Keith and Mark. She thought about calling Cookie but decided against it. Cookie would definitely end up staying the night, and Demisha wanted Keith's full attention. She would tell Cookie all the gossip later.

As Demisha stepped outside and made it down two steps, someone shouted, "Catch!"

She looked up and saw the football coming fast. She threw her hands up, and it hit her fingernail, breaking it. Her finger began bleeding. Holding it, she kicked the football into the neighbor's yard.

Keith came rushing over, apologizing. "You okay? I thought you was ready."

"I'm bleeding here."

Demisha was tough. She and Darren used to fight when they were younger.

"Besides the bloody finger, you looking cute today," Keith said. "What's the occasion?"

Demisha was caught off guard by the comment. Keith was brown-skinned with a small mustache, and his teeth were really white. It made his smile more appealing to her.

"I was coming from a friend's birthday party."

Keith nodded. "Did Mark tell you what I said?"

"He mentioned something."

"You know you and your homegirl Cookie the same height, but built different?"

"How so?"

"Cookie said your butt noticeable. When you jump rope, your butt always stop the rope from turning."

Demisha smiled. "You only see the bottom part?"

"No, I see your cute nose and who's in charge." Keith was feeling confident. "Would you like to get to know me?"

Demisha said, "Okay."

Keith went over, grabbed the football, and threw it to Mark, telling him to give him ten minutes. Mark's big teeth showed as he ran back toward his house.

Keith stepped closer to Demisha.

"Not so close," she said. "My mom's inside."

"Not a problem," Keith said.

He started telling her he was nineteen and wanted to go to college.

"To play football?" Demisha said playfully.

Keith smirked. "You don't think I got talent?"

"Maybe if you practice more."

"I'll keep that in mind. I want a degree in architecture."

"What's that?"

"Have you ever been to Chicago?"

"No."

"If you ever get the chance, ask your brother to take you around downtown. I want to be the person where you look at a building and acknowledge my work."

"You paint too?"

"No, I mean the design and the shape of the building. Take for instance the houses on this street. You see how all these roofs have a certain slope?"

Demisha had never noticed, but now she saw what he meant.

"I'd design something like that. My own signature. I'm part Black and Cuban."

"Cuban?" Demisha asked.

"Yeah. My mother's Cuban, and my father's Black."

They talked until it got dark. Demisha heard her mother calling for her and told Keith she'd see him later.

"Next Saturday," Keith said.

Demisha smiled and went inside.

Every Saturday, they got closer until one night, when Demisha's hormones got the best of her. She told Keith she was ready and wanted him to be her first. After that night, Keith stopped showing up. Demisha would catch Mark outside and ask when the last time he talked to his cousin.

Mark played dumb. "I ain't seen him since I found out about the secret."

"So you know too? He saying it's not his. Do you believe that? You ever seen me with any other boys?"

"No, but he my cousin. Why would I go against that?"

"You sound ignorant." Demisha wanted to punch Mark in his face. If she swung and missed, she'd probably break her hand on his teeth.

Now Mark was avoiding her too. Demisha stayed ready, waiting for the day that van would show up again.

CHAPTER 5

Darren was already dreading the day as he heard the birds chirping. It was Sunday morning, and the weekend had gone by fast. He felt uneasy about the whole trip. They never left the apartment or did any shopping.

For the moment, Darren was all smiles. Kim was resting on his chest. These were the memories Darren loved to cherish, having a strong woman by his side. As Darren thought about Demisha, he noticed an eyeball looking up at him.

"Good morning, love," Kim said.

Darren leaned down and gave her a little peck on the lips. "Somebody got dragon breath."

"Shut up," Kim said. "We both got it."

"While you was getting your beauty sleep, I already brushed my teeth and gargled with mouthwash."

"Now that a lie, because you are very glued to this plush body?"

"Since I'm not mad at you, you can lay in my bed all day."

Darren laughed, then quickly returned to a quiet stare at Kim. Kim knew what that look meant.

At some point, Darren had to get up and pack.

"Do you want me to fix you something to eat?"

"Nah, I'll get a soda on the road."

"How about we just lay here a few more minutes and then

take a shower?"

*

Demisha was scrambling around in the closet, debating what to wear for school on Monday. Cookie was reading an XXL magazine, listening to her best friend complain about having no clothes to wear.

"Maybe Darren could buy me some winter clothes."

"Looking cute is out the window," Cookie said. "You should be thinking about some new maternity clothes."

"I have a few months before that happens." Demisha was trying not to think about the weight gain or wearing big sweaters to hide the baby bump.

"What your brother say about the pregnancy?" Cookie asked.

"He tried calling, but I let it go straight to voicemail. He's going to give me an earful when he gets home."

Demisha and Cookie continued talking when they heard a car horn outside. Cookie jumped up to the window to see who was blowing the horn.

"You see a gray van across the street?" Demisha asked.

"Nah, Del. It's someone down the street."

"You think you'll see Keith again?"

"He'll be back, and I'll be waiting."

*

Darren made sure everything was packed in his overnight bag. He didn't want to waste any time getting back on the highway. Traffic shouldn't be too bad. The sky was clear, no chance of snow, and the sun was hiding behind the clouds.

Darren held Kim's hand as they walked to the parking lot of her apartment. They had a small conversation about their relationship, about living together full-time. Darren wanted Kim to move to Indiana. Kim wanted Darren to move to Michigan. She was already established, and the rent was low. Darren promised her he would think about it.

"You know it gets harder and harder every time I leave," he said.

"I know," Kim said. "We'll work it out together," she added, continuing to hug him.

Darren looked at his watch. It was eleven forty-five a.m.

"I'll be on the road by twelve. Get home around three, maybe."

"Do you need to get gas first?"

"I should be cool, but I'll stop once I get on I-94." Darren opened the car door to his powder blue '84 Pontiac Grand Prix. He gave Kim one long kiss on the lips.

"I love you."

As Darren started the engine, he looked at her. "Maybe you could come to Indiana for a visit."

"Maybe."

"I'll pay for everything."

"Like I was. You still owe."

"Get in the house before you get sick."

Just as Darren was about to put the car in reverse, Kim walked up to the driver's side and leaned in for another kiss. "Call me when you get home."

"I'll call the minute I get to Indiana."

"Love you."

"Love you more." Darren watched as Kim slowly walked back toward the apartment. He tapped the horn, then peeled off.

[illegible]ship, about living together full time. Darren wanted Kim to move to Indiana. Kim wanted Darren to move to Michigan. She was already established and the rent was low. Darren promised he would think about it.

"You know it gets harder and harder every time I leave," he said.

"I know," Kim said. "We'll work it out together," she added, continuing to hug him.

Darren looked at his watch. It was [illegible] forty-five [illegible].

"I'll be on the road by twelve. [illegible] home around [illegible], maybe."

"Do you need to get gas yet?"

"I should be good but I'll get some before I get on I-94," Darren [illegible] down the window [illegible] gave Kim one long kiss on the lips.

"I love you."

As Darren started the engine, he looked at her. "Maybe you could come to Indiana for a visit."

"Maybe."

"I'll pay for everything."

"I'll let you know."

"Get in the house before you get sick."

Just as Darren was about to put the car in reverse, Kim walked up to the driver's side and leaned in for another kiss. "Call me when you get home."

"I'll call the minute I get to Indiana."

"Love you."

"Love you too." Darren watched as Kim slowly walked back toward the apartment. He tapped the horn then pulled off.

CHAPTER 6

Darren had made two stops before he saw the sign that he was entering Michigan City. The first stop was for gas. The second stop gave him a little scare. His check engine light came on.

He immediately made a detour to a truck stop. Darren got out of the car, popped the hood, and checked the oil. Not liking what he saw, he wiped the dipstick and checked it again. He was about two quarts low. Darren went inside the store and asked the cashier where they kept the oil. The cashier pointed toward the back wall. Darren grabbed some WD-40 and paid for the gas and oil.

Back outside, he poured about two and a half quarts of oil into the engine, dropped the hood, and got back on the highway, bumping some Jay-Z from his stereo. After about thirty minutes, he was back in Gary.

"Thank you, Lord, for a safe trip," Darren said quietly.

He looked at his watch. It was a quarter after three. Not bad.

The whole drive, he had been thinking about how to approach the situation with his sister. Should he yell or just listen? There were times when his sister tried to act tough, but deep down, he knew that when a woman is hurting or feels alone, she cries, and Darren knew he would always be there to protect his baby sister.

As he rounded the corner near Ky's house, he thought about stopping to check on him. But it was Sunday, and Ky might not want to be bothered. Instead, Darren kept driving.

He turned onto Broadway, heading toward Glen Park. Once he reached 49th Street, he turned left onto Pennsylvania Street. He found a spot along the curb two houses down from their place. He got out of the car, grabbed his bag, and locked the door behind him.

*

Demisha was already looking out the window when she recognized her brother's car. Once she said it was Darren, Cookie started teasing.

"Ooh, somebody in trouble."

"Do you want me to stay here with you, just in case he get too loud?"

"It's cool, girl. I'll see you at school tomorrow."

"Okay," Cookie said.

Cookie was putting her shoes on when she heard the door open. She stepped out of the room and spoke to Darren. "What's up, big head?"

Darren had a blank stare on his face. He held the door open for her. "You can leave."

Cookie smacked her lips. "Whatever."

As the door closed, Darren looked toward the hallway. "Demisha, come out your room and explain everything to me. You can't hide now. You know how many times I called."

Demisha walked slowly into the living room as Darren kept talking.

"Why would you tell Kim before me?"

"I knew how you would react."

"I was irate. I spent the whole weekend thinking about you. I didn't even get a chance to enjoy myself."

"I'm sorry, bro." The tears started coming. "Keith was stuck on stupid, and I didn't tell Momma."

"You haven't told Momma?"

"Nobody really knows."

"Stop crying. I'm pissed, but I had a lot of time to think on the highway. Whatever you need, I'll help as much as I can. But you have to tell Momma."

"She's still at work. She gets off around midnight."

"I need to get some rest and go to work in the morning," Darren said.

"I need some school clothes," Demisha said.

"I'll think about it. Tell me more about this Keith dude. How come I never saw him?"

"He came mostly on Saturdays. He's Mark's cousin. Big teeth Mark."

"Yeah?"

"It was during the summertime. You'd be gone at work, and Momma would be playing cards with her friends. So I'd be outside chillin' with Cookie... and one thing led to another."

"How old is he?"

"Nineteen."

"I'm twenty. The minute I see him." Darren slammed his fist into his hand.

"There you go. Don't be stupid. Momma not going to bail you out again. I don't want you getting locked up."

Darren had done his time in the county jail. Demisha had seen the change in him since he started working at the shoe store. He hadn't been in trouble with the law since.

"I'm going to the basement to call Kim." Darren stepped forward and hugged his sister. "We're going to sit down as a family and figure this out."

Demisha held onto him a little tighter. "Okay."

As Darren walked toward the basement door, Demisha went back into her room and closed the door.

"You haven't told Momma?"

"Nobody really knows."

"Stop crying. I'm pissed, but I had a lot of time to think on the highway. Whatever you need, I'll help as much as I can. But you have to tell Momma."

"She's still at work. She gets off around midnight."

"I need to get some sleep and go to work in the morning," Darren said.

"I need some school clothes," Demisha said.

"I'll think about it. Tell me more about this Keith dude. How come I never saw him?"

"He came mostly on Saturdays. He's Mecca's cousin. He goes to Mack."

"Yeah?"

"It was during the summertime. You'd be gone to work, and Momma would be playing cards with her friends. She'd be outside chillin' with Cousin [illegible] ... and one thing led to another."

"How old is he?"

"Nineteen."

"Nineteen? The [illegible] I see him," Darren slammed his fist into his hand.

"When you go, don't be stupid. Momma not going to bail you out again. I don't want you getting locked up."

Darren had done his time in the county jail. Demisha had seen the change in him since he started working at the hardware store. He hadn't been in trouble with the law since.

"I'm going to the basement to call Kim." Darren stepped forward and hugged his sister. "We're going to sit down as a family and figure this out."

Demisha held onto him a little tighter. "[illegible]."

As Darren walked toward the basement door, Demisha went back into her room and closed the door.

CHAPTER 7

Debra Owens was sitting in the passenger seat of a black Cadillac DeVille. Robert was Debra's boyfriend, and he had retired from Gary Methodist Hospital, where Debra worked.

Robert put the car in park in front of Debra's house. It was close to one o'clock in the morning. Debra's feet were hurting, and she was ready to lay down.

"What's the rush?" Robert said.

Debra wasn't in the mood at this time of night. Robert had that smooth, rich tone. He carried himself with confidence and was very assertive. Debra turned to face him. Robert had a provocative smile and dark chocolate features. She had to admit, she had a weakness for him. She already knew what he wanted to discuss; it was about moving in with him. He knew she had two kids.

Robert was in his late fifties. He had one older son, but he told Debra he was done raising children. Debra loved her kids, but she knew Darren and Demisha would put a strain between her and Robert. Robert had promised to carry the load, to provide and pay for whatever she needed.

"Robert, how about we talk about this more when I get some rest and when the kids leave the house?"

"I'm not saying move in with me tonight, but sweetheart, I have needs."

"You saying I don't satisfy you?"

"My needs are for you to be by my side. Time is of the essence."

"Goodnight, Robert." Debra opened the door and slammed it. She watched the taillights of the Cadillac as it drove up the street.

When Debra walked inside, the house felt modest and quiet. Darren's shoes were sitting in the middle of the living room. She was too tired to be upset. She went straight to her bedroom and kicked off her work shoes, changed into her nightclothes, and laid down in bed.

*

Demisha had gotten up ten minutes early to get ready for school. Her mother's door was still closed, which meant do not disturb. She made her way toward the basement to see if Darren was up. When she opened the door, she could hear the radio playing softly from his stereo.

"You better keep it down before you wake up Momma."

"What she gon' do? Whoop me?"

"Nah, just kick you out the house. Get ready for school."

"I'm getting ready."

Demisha started to close the door when Darren called out, "Hey!"

"What?"

"After school, come straight home."

"You not my daddy."

"We have to tell Momma about the baby."

"You just wanna see somebody get yelled at."

"I'm being serious. I told you before. I got your back."

Demisha appreciated her brother's support, but she still had doubts about telling her mother.

"I should be home around four," Darren said.

"Fine." Demisha closed the door.

*

Demisha was thinking about what to say to her momma, not paying attention to her math teacher, Ms. Jenkins.

Ma, I'm pregnant. Ma, you're going to be a grandmother. Her eyes drifted back to the clock on the wall, waiting for it to ring.

When the bell finally rang, Demisha closed her algebra book and dashed into the hallway. She moved down the corridor, looking for Cookie. She spotted her talking to Dre, the point guard for the boys' basketball team.

"Hey, Dee," Dre said.

"What's good?" Demisha replied quickly. "I'm sorry, but I need my friend." She grabbed Cookie's hand and pulled her down the hallway.

"Girl, I was trying to give him my digits."

"Do it later. Right now, I'm in crisis mode."

"You told your momma?"

"Not yet. Darren wants us to tell her when he gets home around four."

"Did you take notes in algebra class?" Cookie asked.

"I couldn't concentrate with everything going on." Demisha was distraught.

"Dee, it's going to be all right. You need to talk to Mark and make him lie to get Keith to come."

"Like what?"

"They're cousins. Mark could say your momma threatened to kick you out and that he needs to help you get an apartment."

"Keith doesn't even have a job. He's trying to enroll in college, and I can't wait four or five years for him to get a degree."

They kept talking as the hallway started to clear.

"I gotta get to English," Cookie said. "I'll walk with you after school."

Demisha just nodded as she watched Cookie disappear into the crowd, then she headed to Typing 101.

CHAPTER 8

Demisha and Cookie were leaving school together. Demisha checked the time on her cellphone. It was only five minutes after three. She texted her brother: *Heading home.*

Demisha closed her phone and looked at Cookie. "You mind chilling at the house for a while?"

"No problem," Cookie said.

*

Darren was maintaining a steady pace at work. On this Monday morning, Phil, the part-time warehouse guy, had called in sick. That meant Darren had to unload the shipment by himself. Ky said he had a bad back and couldn't lift anything heavy. All he did was point, raising his finger to where he wanted the boxes placed.

The only words coming out of Darren's mouth were, "Right here?" and "You sure?"

Darren was glad there wasn't much traffic coming in and out of the store. Otherwise, he would've had to stop what he was doing in the back to help customers up front.

He felt a buzz in his pocket. At first, he thought it was Kim, still a little upset that he hadn't called her when he got home. He had told her he lost track of time talking to Demisha. Kim understood and told him to call when he got some free time.

Darren didn't realize it was already after three. He had made a promise to his sister, and he didn't want to come up empty on that. Once everything was in place and every shoebox was where it belonged, Ky seemed satisfied.

"You did a good job," Ky said. "Maybe one day I'll take a day off and let you be the manager."

"I practically run this shop, Ky. Think about it. Take a day off. Let me show you how responsible I can be."

Ky just smiled, then walked into his office and closed the door.

Darren knew Ky was set in his ways. The man never took days off. The store was all he had, and he wasn't ready to let it go. Since things were slow, Darren figured he could leave now and make it home by four.

He knocked on the glass window and gestured to Ky that he was heading out. Ky waved him off. Darren grabbed his red hoodie and took off.

*

Demisha slowly opened the door as she stepped inside the house. She instantly smelled chicken grease coming from the kitchen, which meant her momma was cooking lunch for work. Chicken and macaroni: her favorite.

Demisha turned around and whispered, "She here!"

"You want me to come inside?" Cookie asked.

"Darren should be here. Whatever happens, stay by your phone."

"Okay," Cookie said, heading back home.

Demisha stepped further inside just as Debra came out of the kitchen. They locked eyes.

"What's wrong?" Debra asked.

"Nothing."

"How was school?"

"School was okay."

"I left you and your brother some chicken and mac."

"Thanks, Momma."

"I'm going to lay down before Robert comes to pick me up for work."

Demisha had heard of Robert but had never met him.

As Debra walked into her room and closed the door, Demisha heard the key turn in the front door.

Darren stepped inside, brushing off the cold. It seemed like the weather was getting colder. He saw Demisha standing in the living room.

"Where Momma?"

"She just went in her room to take a nap."

"Go knock on the door."

Demisha shook her head.

"Stop playin'," Darren said. "Go ahead."

"She going to get mad."

"Well, we said today at four. It's four-fifteen. I'm here for you."

Demisha took her bookbag off her shoulder and slowly walked toward her momma's door.

CHAPTER 9

Demisha knocked on the door twice. “Ma.”

She knocked again.

From behind the door, Debra yelled, “I’m trying to sleep!”

Demisha didn’t back down. “Me and Darren need to talk to you.”

Darren stepped closer. “It’s important, Ma.”

They heard footsteps approaching. The door swung open, and Debra stood there with a deep frown. “What’s so important?” she asked.

Darren took the lead. “Can we talk in the kitchen?”

“I’ve been in the kitchen all morning cooking. I’m trying to relax in my own house, in my own bed. Tell me what the problem is.”

“I don’t have the problem,” Darren said. “But as a family, we should come together.”

Debra’s eyes shifted from Darren to Demisha. Demisha looked at her brother, but no words came out.

Debra stepped forward. Demisha took two steps back until they were standing face to face in the living room. Debra was slightly bigger, but Demisha was taller.

Demisha was nervous. “I think a drink of water will help me.”

Debra blocked her path. “Whatever you got to say, say it. I don’t have time for games. And don’t lie.”

Demisha looked at Darren.

"Don't look at him," Debra snapped. "Spit it out!"

"I'm pregnant, Mom."

Darren's reaction was too slow. Debra's hand came fast, striking Demisha across the face. The slap echoed through the living room, knocking her onto the couch.

Demisha screamed. "She crazy! Darren, help!"

Darren grabbed his mother, trying to hold her back as she kept yelling.

"You're not staying here! You ruined your life!"

"I'm sorry!" Demisha cried.

"Mom, fighting isn't the answer," Darren said. "She your daughter."

Debra turned on him. "I'm the parent. You shut up!"

"I can't do that, Ma. She my sister."

Debra swung at Darren, but he blocked her. He would never raise his hand against his mother.

"All I do is work and do what's best for my kids," Debra shouted. "Your daddy was never around. I've been doing this on my own!"

"Ma, we know that."

"Do you?" she snapped. "Who the daddy? Is it that boy Mark across the street?"

"No!" Demisha sobbed.

"Who the daddy, girl?"

"His cousin... Keith."

"Who is Keith?"

"He lives in Chicago."

Debra kept yelling. "You kids are never content. Y'all make my life a living hell. I got a man ready to give me a good life, and I told him my kids come first. But this how y'all repay me? Getting pregnant, in and out of jail, living in my basement."

Darren started to speak, then stopped. He knew it would only make things worse.

"I want a happy life," Debra continued. "And Robert might be the man for me."

Darren felt that one.

Debra pointed at Demisha. "The minute you walk across that stage, I want you out this house."

"Mom—"

"Darren, stay out of this!"

Demisha jumped up and ran out the house. Behind her, she could still hear Debra yelling.

"Don't come back!"

Demisha ran to Cookie. The one person she trusted.

*

The next day, the Owens house was quiet. Darren sat in the basement, struggling with his emotions. Debra had left for work without saying a word. Demisha texted him that she would be staying at Cookie's place for a couple of days. Darren promised to bring her bookbag and some clothes.

He didn't feel like going to work, but he knew it would help keep his mind steady, and he might need the money. Demisha was going to need support. Darren sat on the edge of his bed, planning his next move, when his phone rang.

Kim.

He answered in a low tone.

"Hello? Darren, can you hear me?" Kim asked.

"Yeah."

"What's up?"

"I was just calling. I was thinking about you."

"Thanks. Can I call you back, Kim?"

Kim paused. She could tell something was off. "What's the matter, bae?"

"So much is going on. I just need time to think."

"When something's wrong, we talk it out. We communicate."

"Yeah, you right," Darren said. "Maybe you can give me a different perspective. Between my mother and my sister."

"Talk to me," Kim said.

CHAPTER 10

Darren confided in Kim while getting ready for work. He told her everything: the fight between Debra and Demisha, how his mom felt like she couldn't live the life she wanted.

"She feels trapped, Kim. And I'm hurting."

Kim could hear Darren getting choked up, trying to talk through it.

"It's going to be difficult for me to come see you before Christmas. Maybe next year, just until we get over this hump. I would love for you to be here with me."

Kim was quiet on the phone. She wondered if this would put a strain on their relationship. She had already decided she would go the distance for Darren. He had earned her trust.

"If you need me, sweetheart, then I'm coming."

"I couldn't ask you to do that, Kim."

"You've got my heart, and that's not easy to do. We going through a rough start, but it'll get easier."

There was a pause.

"My sister Nisha can stay at the apartment for a couple of weeks. I'm getting on the next train to Indiana. Christmas is coming early for you, so wipe that snot from your nose and get things in order."

Darren laughed. "No snot. Just a few tears."

"Call me back with all the information on the time I get

there."

"I got to go. I'm running late for work," Darren said.

"Love you."

"Love you too," Kim said.

Darren grabbed his keys, a smile on his face.

Kim was coming for him.

*

Demisha was in Cookie's bathroom as they got ready for school. She stared at the bruises on her hands and arms from the fight with her momma. She was still dumbfounded by Debra's reaction.

Am I a bad child?

Getting pregnant was the one mistake Debra couldn't let go.

When Demisha opened the bathroom door, she looked at Cookie. "Can you braid my hair? And you got a sweater I can use?"

"Anything you can find," Cookie said. "Just don't stretch my sweater out."

"What you mean? We about the same size."

"For now, but when that baby come—"

"Don't even start," Demisha said.

Cookie was trying to lighten the mood, but she could see the pain in her friend's face.

"When you thinking about going back home?"

"I don't know. Let me text Darren and see if he can bring my bookbag and some clothes up to the school."

"Your momma won't be trippin' that I'm here?" Demisha asked.

"Girl, we got plenty of room. Plus, my mom know we like sisters. Now sit still and see if I can braid this mess."

They both started laughing.

*

Darren was helping a customer when he felt his phone buzz. After thanking the customer for shopping at the Nike Factory, he checked it, thinking it was Kim.

It was Demisha. She was asking about her bookbag and clothes. Darren had completely forgotten. He'd been so caught up earlier, talking to Kim.

The house had been quiet. The couch was still out of place from the fight. He hadn't even bothered fixing anything. He'd deal with it later. Hopefully, his momma would be home so they could talk. And beyond that, he was thinking about something else.

How Debra would react when Kim showed up.

Would she let Kim stay in the basement with him? Or would it turn into another fight? Darren headed to the back and asked Ky if he could take his lunch break early.

Darren was helping a customer when he felt his phone buzz. After thanking the customer for shopping at the Bike Factory, he checked [illegible] it was Kim.

It was Ayanisha. She was asking about her bookbag and clothes. Darren had completely forgotten. He'd been so caught up earlier [illegible].

The bookbag had been [illegible]. The [illegible] was still [illegible] of [illegible] from the fight. [illegible] to [illegible] Ayanisha [illegible] would [illegible] they could [illegible]. And [illegible] that [illegible] working [illegible] something [illegible].

How [illegible] would [illegible]?

Would she let Kim stay in the basement with him? Or would it turn into another fight? Darren headed to the back and [illegible] he could take his lunch break early.

CHAPTER 11

Kim was packing her suitcase for the trip to Indiana. Her sister Nisha would be at the apartment in twenty minutes to take her to the train station in Dearborn. Her train left at twelve-thirty and would arrive around five.

Kim texted Darren the details. *Don't be late. Love you.*

She made sure she packed all her combs and hair products. Kim was a full-time braider, working out of her home. She called a few of her clients and told them she had a family emergency and would be out of town for a couple of weeks.

Kim planned to keep herself busy in Indiana, maybe make some money, and help Darren however she could. She double-checked her bags before leaving. Before heading out, she reminded Nisha not to have any company in the apartment. Just her and the baby.

Kim had never left Michigan before and she was anxious and excited. But one thing she knew for sure: she was in love with Darren.

*

Darren didn't waste any time on his lunch break. He made it home quickly to grab Demisha's bookbag and some clothes. Before locking up, he noticed his mother still wasn't home.

Demisha had texted him to meet her and Cookie at the gas station down the street from the high school.

When Darren pulled up, Demisha and Cookie came out of the store. Darren hopped out and handed his sister her bag.

"Thanks," Demisha said, giving her big brother a hug.

"You coming home after school?" Darren asked.

"Not right away. I want to stay at Cookie's house a few more days."

Darren nodded. "Momma didn't come home this morning." He reached into his back pocket, pulled out some money, and handed Demisha fifty dollars.

"Thanks for letting her stay at your crib," Darren said to Cookie.

"That's my girl," Cookie replied.

"You can sit in the car and warm up," Darren said. "I need a minute with her."

Cookie walked over to the car and got in the driver's seat.

Darren looked at Demisha's head. "You went to school like that?"

"Like what?"

"Your hair."

"Cookie did her best."

Darren looked toward the car and waved at Cookie, motioning toward Demisha's hair. Cookie looked up and gave him the middle finger. Darren laughed, then got serious again. "Kim coming to Indiana for a few weeks."

"To do what?"

"To help me and meet the family."

Demisha nodded slowly.

"Since Momma didn't come home, I'm going to catch her at work," Darren continued. "Then head straight to the train station."

"You think she calmed down?" Demisha asked.

"I hope so. She might get upset when Kim shows up."

"What time she get here?"

"Five."

"I'm going to try to catch Momma before her shift starts."

"Well, me and Cookie about to get something to eat and head back to school. After school, if your car at the house, I might stop by."

"All right," Darren said. "Text me later."

"I will." Demisha hugged her brother again, then walked over to the car to get Cookie.

CHAPTER 12

Darren was trying to rush out of the shoe store. Ky wanted him to stay and close.

"I gotta go pick up my girl from the train station and deal with some things at home," Darren said.

Ky looked at him. "You the one that wanted manager duties. Show me the leader that you are."

Darren knew what Ky was doing.

"Today not that day, Ky. We can hammer out the details tomorrow." With that, Darren left.

He got into his car and headed toward the hospital. The time on his phone read 4:20. He could make it there in fifteen minutes. Darren didn't have high expectations for the conversation. His mother's emotions always came out as anger, never affection.

He made a right turn on Broadway and pulled toward the back entrance of Gary Methodist, hoping to catch her before her shift started. As he drove up, a black Cadillac passed by. Darren pressed the gas, heading up the ramp. He saw Debra waving to a few people as she walked toward the entrance. Darren hit the horn twice.

Debra turned her head, saw his car and kept walking.

Darren jumped out, leaving the car running. "Mom!"

He ran toward the entrance, waiting for the doors to slide open. Once they did, he rushed inside, catching up to her. "Mom, wait!"

Debra stopped, but didn't turn around.

Darren stepped in front of her. "Why didn't you come home after work?"

"I don't have to tell you anything."

"I was worried about you."

"Don't worry about me. I'm grown."

Darren took a breath. "Look, I came here to talk about Demisha."

"There's nothing to talk about." Her voice started to rise.

"She your daughter. Her graduation coming up. We need you at home."

"Robert needs me at his home."

Darren stared at her. "You really believe that? He playing you, Mom."

Debra's hand came fast. The slap cracked across Darren's face in the waiting area. Nobody was around.

"Like I said, Robert needs me. You and your sister grown. Take care of each other. I'm doing what's best for Debra." She walked past him.

Darren stood there, rubbing his jaw.

*

The train from Dearborn, Michigan, was arriving in Hammond, Indiana at 5:10 p.m. Kim was nervous. The ride had been nice and quiet. She had fallen asleep twice, waking up to admire the scenery: trees and open land rushing past the window.

The conductor walked down the aisle. "Next stop, Hammond, Indiana."

Kim's ears perked up. *This is it.* She was ready for whatever she had to face: a new chapter in her life. *Is Darren the guy for me? Will he change? Will he be that perfect gentleman?*

As the train began to slow, Kim stared out the window, searching for him.

Darren barely made it to the station by 5:13. He could hear the train horn blowing loud. The red lights were already flashing, but with no other trains coming, he drove around the crossing guard and across the tracks. Once he stepped out of the car, he pulled his skull cap down over his ears against the cold. He stood there, watching each passenger step off the train. Darren felt anxious, happy, and heavy at the same time. He still had to tell Kim the truth. She wouldn't be meeting his mother anytime soon. Everything was on him now.

He walked closer to the station. Then he saw Kim. She was walking toward him, waving. Beautiful. She came all this way to support him. How could he ever mistreat her?

Darren wrapped his arms around her, holding her tight, as if it were the first time they'd met. Kim kissed his cheek, then his lips. Darren laughed as her lip balm left his lips glossy.

"How was the trip?" Darren asked.

"For my first time, it was okay."

"Grab my bag," Kim said, pointing to her big purple luggage.

"My back already hurting," Darren joked.

"Stop crying and be a man," Kim said, smiling.

Darren helped her into the passenger seat, then loaded the luggage into the trunk.

Once they hit the highway, Kim started talking about the train ride, about what she saw, about the city. Darren stayed quiet.

"Bae, you hear me?"

"Mmm... what you say?"

"I said I'm hungry. What you want?"

"I got a taste for fish."

"How about a double cheeseburger?"

"I'm tired of burgers. I want something different."

"No problem."

Darren went quiet again.

"Where your sister at?"

Darren didn't answer.

"Darren."

"Huh?"

"Why you acting like I'm not in the car?"

"I'm just trying to gather my thoughts."

"I didn't know I was disturbing you," Kim said.

"You not." Darren reached for her hand. Kim pulled hers away. "What's wrong, Kim?"

"You tell me."

Darren exhaled. "I want to be honest with you before we get to the house. I went to the hospital to see my momma before picking you up." He paused. "Short version. She not coming back home. She left me and my sister to be with some dude named Robert. She slapped me, and she not coming to Demisha's graduation."

Kim slowly reached for his hand. Darren grabbed it and held tight. "Whatever it takes, I'm here."

"You promise?"

"I promise, love."

CHAPTER 13

Darren and Kim were dressed in all black, sitting in the gymnasium of Lew Wallace High School with hundreds of parents, all waiting for this moment: graduation day.

It had been a rough eight months. Darren had been spending more time at work. Ky let him run the daily operations at the store, which meant more money for the family. Kim had been by Darren's side through it all. She stayed for a month, went back to Michigan for two weeks, then returned for Demisha's graduation.

Kim had been using her skills at the house, taking on a few clients at the Owens residence. Demisha and Cookie had spread the word around school. Kim had spent three hours braiding both their hair for the ceremony.

Darren looked around, still hoping Debra would show up. But deep down, he knew she wasn't coming.

He turned his attention back to the podium as the crowd began to clap.

Principal Dean Fox stepped up. "We welcome you, parents here today for this occasion. We are very proud of our students. Always put education first, and your future will be bright. Here is the class of 2000."

The audience erupted: clapping, whistling, cheering.

"When we call your name, please step forward and receive your diploma."

Darren and Kim waited patiently as the names were called one by one. After about twenty names, they heard it.

"Demisha Owens."

Darren and Kim jumped to their feet, cheering and shouting her name.

Demisha walked across the stage, looking beautiful and very pregnant. There was no hiding her stomach anymore.

A couple of names later—

"Jerica Jackson."

Darren spotted Cookie walking across the stage, and they cheered for her too. He leaned back in his seat, ready to go. The gym was hot, and he was already thinking about the buffet.

*

Darren, Kim, Demisha, and Cookie were laughing and enjoying themselves at the Chinese buffet. Cookie's mom had left after graduation and told her not to stay out too late.

Darren stood up and tapped his glass. "I got an announcement to make."

He looked at Demisha.

"To my baby sister. I just want to say how incredibly proud I am of you. And, um..." Darren paused, getting a little emotional. "Despite all the ups and downs, you'll always be loved. So me and Kim want to give you something."

Kim reached into her purse and pulled out an envelope, handing it to Demisha.

Demisha looked shocked as she took the white envelope and opened it. Inside was a check for three thousand dollars. Demisha jumped up with joy and hugged Kim. "Thank you!" She turned to Darren and whispered, "I love you."

Darren gave her a nod. "Don't spend it on yourself. That's for you and the baby." He looked over at Cookie. "And we want to say thank you to Cookie too."

Everyone raised their glasses of water toward her.

Cookie smiled, trying to play it cool.

"I'm full," Darren said.

Everyone laughed as they gathered their things and got ready to leave the restaurant.

*

As Darren pulled along the curb to park the Buick, he was getting sleepy. He couldn't wait to take a shower and lie down.

"This was a perfect day," Darren said.

They had just dropped off Cookie, and Demisha promised to call her the next day.

As they started walking toward the house, Demisha heard someone calling her name. She turned and saw Mark walking across the street.

It was late, and Demisha just wanted to kick off her heels. Mark picked up his pace, still calling her name.

Darren's mood shifted. *Why is Mark out here this late... waiting for us?*

Demisha noticed something in Mark's hands.

"Hold up!" Mark said.

Darren stayed right by her side. "What you want?"

"I just wanted to congratulate Demisha."

Mark held up some black and gold balloons. "I got a gift for you." He revealed a long black box.

"We don't want nothing from you," Darren said, getting irritated.

"I didn't come over here for an argument," Mark replied. "How about you tell me where your cousin at?"

"I can't control his actions, but he did want Demisha to have this."

"Take it back," Darren said.

"Chill," Demisha told her brother.

Kim stepped in. "Darren, come on. Open the door."

Darren looked at her, unsure.

"Let her handle it," Kim said. "She a big girl."

Darren hesitated, then walked up the steps and opened the door. "Don't be long."

Demisha turned back to Mark. "This from Keith?"

"He had to leave. He wanted you to have that."

"What is it?"

"Just open it."

Demisha took the box and opened it. Inside was an eighteen-karat gold bracelet.

"It's nice," she said quietly. "Tell him thank you."

She grabbed the balloons, then let them go, watching them drift into the sky. As she walked up the steps, she looked back at Mark. "It's his baby." Demisha stepped inside and closed the door. The moment it shut, she broke down crying.

Kim saw her and rushed over. "You okay?"

Demisha held out her hand. Kim took it.

"What's wrong?"

Kim's eyes dropped and froze.

A dark, wet stain spread across Demisha's gown. "I think the baby's coming."

"Darren!" Kim yelled.

CHAPTER 14

On June ninth, at a quarter past one in the morning, Darren and Kim welcomed a six-pound, healthy baby girl into the family.

Darren was relieved the yelling had finally stopped. Demisha was exhausted from pushing and had already fallen asleep. He stood there, watching his niece cry as the nurse checked her vitals.

Darren was finally able to hold her. She had a yellow tone to her skin and soft, curly black hair.

"She so cute," Kim said. "She look like a little butterscotch."

"That's a cute nickname," Darren said. "I'm going to call her that."

Darren told Kim to grab the camera.

"Say uncle," Kim said.

"Uncle," Darren smiled, just as the flash went off.

Demisha stirred awake. "Let me see my baby."

Darren carefully walked over and placed the baby in her arms.

Demisha looked up at her brother and whispered, "Did Momma show up?"

They were at Methodist Hospital, where Debra worked.

Darren slowly shook his head.

Demisha leaned back against the pillow, holding her baby girl close.

"We nicknamed her Butterscotch," Kim said. "But what name you putting on the birth certificate?"

Demisha looked down at her daughter. "I already had a name picked out," she said softly. "Kameesha."

*

On a warm, sunny day, Darren and the family pulled up to the house. Demisha and Kameesha were in the backseat of the Buick. After four days of rest, Demisha was finally leaving the hospital.

Debra never showed up to meet her grandbaby.

Darren told Demisha to be careful as she got Kameesha out of the car seat. Kim grabbed the overnight bag and held the door as Demisha stepped out. Kameesha was asleep.

"Welcome home, baby girl," Demisha whispered.

As they walked into the house, Darren glanced across the street. No van. No Mark.

Mark was watching from his living room window. He knew Darren couldn't see him, but he had a feeling who Darren was looking for. As he watched them go inside, Mark picked up the phone and called his cousin.

"Just to let you know, Demisha had the baby," Mark said.

"Are you sure?" Keith asked.

"Yeah, man. She just carried the baby inside."

There was a pause.

"Do me a favor."

"What's that, cuz?"

"When you get a chance, tell me if she look like me."

"I'll try my best," Mark said.

CHAPTER 15

Over the next several years, Demisha was a good mother to Kameesha. Everyone continued to pitch in to babysit and help Demisha stay focused. Kim was a mentor to Demisha, teaching her how to use her fingers for the underhand technique of braiding cornrows during the day. And at night, Demisha pursued her cosmetology license.

Darren gave his Buick to Demisha so she could get back and forth. Demisha gave the car back because it wasn't girly enough. Auntie Cookie came over to help with Kameesha after her shift at the Indiana State Prison. Cookie would rock Kameesha back and forth in her arms as Demisha braided Cookie's hair.

"Girl, your skills are getting better than mine. Don't braid too tight in the back. I don't want to walk around at work all day with a headache."

"I got you," Demisha said.

"So, tell me your latest gossip from prison."

"What makes you think I got a story?"

"You always do. I need to laugh."

"Them fools at Michigan City are funny. You know the average convict claims they could get rich in one day. There was one guy who was cute in the face, but had dandruff in his hair, trying to talk to me while scratching his head. Girl, I'd be shaking my uniform after I left him. Most guys barely had a hundred dollars on their accounts. Maybe a family member was holding that cash. Don't know. Don't care."

"You remember Dre from high school? That used to be on the basketball team?"

"Yeah."

"He was there serving ten years for dealing. He still looked good. He told me to wait for him."

"Are you?" Demisha said.

"Heck no."

Demisha started laughing. "I'd be an old woman by then. Do you get scared sometimes?"

"Not really. You have some weirdos, but a girl will fight if she has to. I'm just trying to get a paycheck."

*

Later on that night, Darren was walking down the basement steps. He was holding some baby shoes.

"Kim, check these out. All pink baby Converse."

Darren noticed Kim's posture, as if something was wrong.

"What's the matter?"

"I feel like the room is spinning down here. We need our own apartment," Kim said.

Darren knew at some point this discussion would come up.

"I would agree with you, but since Debra left, and now the baby, I don't think Demisha is ready for this type of responsibility."

"I'm not your basic girlfriend coming and leaving, Darren. I been ridin' with you for a couple of years. I understand you want to be protective of Demisha and Kameesha. Are you ready to start your own family?"

Kim rose up from the bed and walked toward Darren.

"I'm not expecting a big house, but something we can call our home."

Darren put his arms around Kim's waist.

"Umm, that was a mouthful. How long have you been thinking about this?"

"The day I left Michigan."

"I'm not promising anything right now."

Kim was trying to wiggle out of Darren's hands.

"Wait, I'm not done. Kameesha birthday is coming up. She be turning four. We can look at a few apartment buildings around here."

"That cool," Kim said, smiling and turning around to look Darren in his eyes.

"I just have to find a way to tell Demisha," Darren said.

CHAPTER 16

"Happy birthday to you, happy birthday to you. Happy birthday to Kameesha."

Demisha had a special SpongeBob SquarePants ice cream cake with the number four in the middle of the cake. Darren took pictures as Kim, Cookie, and Demisha helped Butterscotch blow out the candles.

Everyone shouted, "Yeah!" when all the candles went out. Kameesha was clapping from all the excitement.

Demisha wanted to keep the party simple: only family. She wasn't ready to have a whole bunch of kids running around in the house from Kameesha's school.

Darren told Demisha he needed to talk and let Auntie Cookie cut the cake. He led Demisha into the hallway from the living room.

"What's up, Uncle D?" Demisha said.

Darren leaned back on the wall. "There's something I need to tell you."

"Tell me what?"

"Me and Kim is going to start looking for our own spot."

Unexpectedly, Demisha punched Darren in his arm. "For what, stupid?"

Kim saw what transpired and continued to watch Kameesha eat her cake.

Rubbing his arm, Darren said, "Not right away. But I'm getting pressured. Kim feel trapped in the basement."

Demisha tried to keep her voice down. "Walking out on your family? Kameesha is adjusted to having y'all here. Can you wait until I finish school?"

"Now, wait a minute, sis. Don't be disrespectful. I love my family."

"I'm the one here. Remember that."

Darren knew he just opened a wound, and now he felt upset for speaking about their mother. "You know what? I'll be back."

"Where you going?"

Darren was heading for the front door.

Demisha continued to follow her brother. "Darren, come back!"

Even Kim was calling Darren, but Darren didn't stop to listen to anybody. Everyone just watched as the front door slammed.

*

Darren pulled up to the tall apartment complex off Jackson St. He could see Robert's Cadillac standing out on the side curb. Robert's place wasn't that far from the hospital.

Darren's emotions were riding high. It was Kameesha's birthday, and she had never met her grandmother. Darren wanted to repair the relationship between Debra and Demisha. Demisha was going to need some support once Kim and he moved out.

Darren glanced at the intercom system and saw Robert Morris' name. Apartment 2C. He entered the complex and walked up the steps. The building only had three floors, two doors on each floor. Darren found 2C and knocked on the painted red door. He knocked several times before the door opened.

Darren stared at Robert, who was standing over him.

"How can you say that with a straight face? We will always need you."

"Thanks for stopping by, but we got to go."

Darren pushed the door back open. "When you going to grow up and stop acting like this?"

"You need to leave," Robert said.

"Make me leave."

Debra was now between Robert and Darren.

"All I'm asking is my mother to come home."

Darren was sizing Robert up. "Nobody afraid of you."

Robert went into his waist and pulled out a .38 special.

"Put that away," Debra said.

Darren charged Robert, and Debra was screaming for Darren to stop. She grabbed Darren's shoulder.

That's when the gun went off.

Debra was shot in the stomach. Shocked at what happened, Debra fell to the floor.

Darren was holding the gun and told Robert that he killed his momma.

Robert had a grin on his face. "Ain't no loss to me. She can be replaced."

Darren was irate at Robert's comment and pulled the trigger.

"Thanks for stopping by, but we gotta go."

Darren pushed the door back open. "When you going to grow up and stop acting like this?"

"You need to leave," Robert said.

"Make me leave."

Debra was now between Robert and Darren.

"All I'm asking is my mother to come home."

Darren was staring Robert up. "Nobody afraid of you."

Robert went in his jacket and pulled out a .38 special.

"Put that away," Debra said.

Darren lunged at Robert, and Debra was screaming for Darren to stop. She grabbed Darren's shoulder.

That's when the gun went off.

Debra was shot in the stomach. Shocked at what just happened, Darren fell to the floor.

Darren was holding the gun and told everyone that he killed his momma.

Robert had a frown on his face. "Ain't no loss to me. She can be replaced."

[illegible] was able to [illegible] Robert [illegible] and pulled the trigger.

CHAPTER 17

After eight months in the Lake County Jail in Crown Point, Indiana, Darren Owens walked into courtroom number two to hear his fate.

Judge Wilson spoke to the lead prosecutor, Mrs. King. "I understand there is a plea agreement on both sides today."

"Yes, we do, Your Honor," Mrs. King said.

Darren stood up in his orange jumpsuit next to his public defender, Mr. Hodge.

The public defender stated to Judge Wilson that his client would like to make a statement.

"The defendant, Mr. Owens, you may begin whenever you're ready," Judge Wilson said.

Darren did a quick glance at Kim and Demisha as they were sitting silently.

"My actions have caused my family great pain, Your Honor. Growing up with no father, and my mother, Debra Owens, will never know how much I miss her. She was a woman of pride and strength. The boyfriend, Mr. Morris, took my mother away from me and my sister. That's all I have to say, Your Honor."

Judge Wilson flipped through the pages that the court had filed and made some mental notes: in and out of jail, theft, assault. After a few more minutes, the judge was ready to speak.

"Mr. Owens, please stand. On the count of manslaughter,

how do you plead?"

"Guilty, Your Honor."

"Despite your mother being innocent in this crime, I'm sorry she had to lose her life in that manner. You could have made a better choice in regard to Robert Morris. The fact is, you took a life. If I could give you more time, I would. Let this be a lesson for you to reflect on your issues and to make better decisions in your future."

"Mr. Owens, I will sentence you to no more than thirty years in prison. Take the time to heal, and I don't want to see you in my courtroom again." Judge Wilson banged his gavel.

Kim and Demisha were crying in the courtroom as Darren was led away by a court officer.

Darren locked eyes with Demisha and mouthed the words, "I will call you."

*

Demisha's phone rang.

"Hello."

"You have a collect call from... Darren. Press one to accept the call."

"Sis, can you hear me?"

"Yeah. What you need, bro?"

"I need you to talk with Cookie, okay?"

"For what?"

"I can't say everything right now, but tell her to be lookin' out for me."

"All right. How you feeling?"

"Been better, okay. Let me speak to Kim."

Demisha handed the phone to Kim as she was driving.

"Tell your brother to call later. We should be at the house in twenty minutes."

Demisha told her brother.

"Did you hear that?"

"Yeah."

Darren could detect the anger in Kim's voice.

*

By the time Kim was pulling up to the house, her phone was ringing. Kim was getting agitated.

"I can't even get inside the house before he calling me."

Kim answered the phone.

Demisha was closing the door to the Malibu when she heard Mark calling her name.

Kim told Darren, "Let me get inside before I start screaming."

As Kim was walking toward the house, Mark was walking up to Demisha in a police uniform.

"What is this?"

"I'm in training now."

"To do what, security?"

"No, I joined the Gary Police Department."

"To serve this community right," Demisha said in a joking manner.

"Something like that," Mark said. "But I came over here to say sorry for your brother and your mom also. And I wanted to give you this."

Mark handed Demisha a yellow envelope.

Demisha looked inside and saw a whole bunch of twenty-dollar bills.

"How much is this?"

"Five hundred."

"Is this from Keith?"

"No. But I just wanted to help out, despite how my cousin has been treating you. Truth is, and I shouldn't be telling you, you just have to navigate life without him. He got another family. I mean, he was with someone else before he met you, and he couldn't be honest with you upfront, Demisha."

Demisha wanted to throw the money back at Mark.

"If I wasn't going through this mess right now, I would tell you to keep the money and tell your cousin to never speak to me or Kameesha. His flesh and blood." Demisha turned around and walked toward the house.

"If you ever need something, I'm here!" Mark shouted.

"Oh, it like that?" Kim said. "You got an attitude."

"I been trying to apologize, sweetheart. Darren, you realize thirty is a lot of years."

"It's not thirty. I only have to do half of that."

"Well, fifteen ain't no walk in the park either. Who's going to wait that long?"

"You my woman, right?"

"Darren, okay. This is '05, and you want me to stay around until 2020? This is too much for me. All the sacrifice I made for you. I was devoted to you, Darren. Didn't I move to Indiana? Which was supposed to be a few weeks turned into years. So don't go there."

"What happened to the promise, Kim? I got you."

"Yeah, I did say that, Darren. I got you. Not you and prison."

"Will you stay for me?"

"I don't know."

"Wow."

"You know what? Go back to Detroit or wherever you came from. Hit the road, Jack."

Darren slammed the phone.

The COs were saying it was count time.

CHAPTER 18

Kameesha was playing with her toys as Demisha was sitting at the kitchen table thinking. Bills. Bills. Kameesha needs clothes. Kim left. Darren need money.

Just as Demisha was in thought, one of Kameesha's toys hit Demisha's foot. "Come here, Kameesha."

Kameesha walked over toward her mommy.

Demisha smacked Kameesha's hand. "Keep your toys in the living room."

Kameesha started crying and walked away.

Demisha's phone rang.

"Hello?"

"Hey, it's Cookie."

"What's wrong?"

"Nothing, just Kameesha acting out."

"Just wanted to give you a heads up. Your brother will be arriving here later today."

"Treat him right, Cookie."

"I will do my best, sis."

"All right, call me later when you get off. I think we need to go out to a club. I need to release some stress."

"That's cool," Cookie said. "Check you later."

*

Darren was looking at the tall brick wall of Indiana State Prison in Michigan City as he walked into the release and receiving building for inmates. That's when C.O. Jackson told inmate Owens to follow her. Jackson told Owens to keep up.

C.O. Jackson asked Ms. Pearl which dorm.

Ms. Pearl told her E Dorm as they were leaving.

As they got a little distance, Cookie told Darren, "In prison, you must mind your business. Don't worry about anybody else."

"It's the same as juvie," Darren said.

"Times are different, Darren," Cookie said. "I told your sister I will do my best."

Darren asked Cookie, "Can you deliver a message to Demisha?"

"What that?"

"Tell her to send me the picture of the birthday party when Kameesha turn four."

"No problem, Darren. I will check with you on my shift. Keep your head down."

Darren blocked out all the noise as he entered the dorm.

*

Demisha was having a good time at the club called Hole in the Wall. Since Cookie was too tired to hang out, Demisha told Cookie to babysit as she left to have a few drinks and dance with her new friend named Cash.

Cash was six-four, all muscle, with a clean, caramel bald head. Demisha thought he was a pro wrestler. Cash told Demisha that he owned a body repair shop. Demisha told Cash that she had her brother's '84 Buick just sitting. She needed some cash and was willing to sell it.

As Demisha continued to grind on Cash on the dance floor,

Cash whispered into Demisha's ear that he was eager to buy the car and to find out where she lived.

Demisha told Cash to drive her Malibu, and let's finish dancing at her house.

CHAPTER 19

At ten years old, Kameesha continued to observe her mommy's new friends come over at night time and leave early in the morning. Her mom always partied on the weekend.

Kameesha used to watch from her bedroom, the door cracked open. Loud music and older men would laugh loud, and smoke would float in the air.

At times before school, Kameesha would open her mother's bedroom door to see her mother laying in the bed, passed out. Kameesha would constantly shake her mommy to wake up.

"Mommy, I need lunch money."

Demisha would always slur her words. "Wake me... later. Or ask Auntie Cookie."

Kameesha often stared at the picture of her Uncle Darren and her mommy on the nightstand. Her mommy seemed so happy before her uncle went away.

When her mommy would roll over and go back to sleep, Kameesha would check her mommy's stash spot in the drawer. There would be only spare change at the bottom, never any large bills.

Kameesha counted out two dollars in quarters. She put the change in her pocket and closed her mommy's door. Kameesha grabbed her bookbag and headed to school.

*

During the years, Darren kept a routine to stay mentally strong: working out, reading, and completing any programs that the prison had to offer. He had seen his share of violence: war between rival gangs, stabbings, and fights with certain staff members that came to work with a bad attitude.

Darren met a few people inside his dorm. One particular black youngster named Pat That Thing. Darren refused to call him that. He would rob the weaker guys on commissary day. He would carry their laundry bag and sucker punch the guy. Knocked out cold, Pat That Thing would snatch the bag. That's how he survived day to day in this environment.

Many times Darren would think about Kim and wonder what she was up to. He wrote a few letters, but never sent them. Once a week he wrote two letters; one to Demisha and the other to Kameesha. Demisha never wrote back.

Most of the time, he would ask Cookie if everything was okay at the house. Cookie had told Darren about how his sister had different dudes coming in and out of the house, but assured him that she kept an eye on Kameesha, making sure she had clothes for school and food in the house.

"The only thing that girl like is cherry Pop-Tarts."

Darren would smile at that.

Cookie complained about Demisha drinking and partying all night. Darren told Cookie to keep the family together until he came home.

After pulling an all-night shift, Mark would always park along the curb close to the middle school. He would keep a close watch for Kameesha as she crossed the street to school.

Kameesha would always wave.

Mark admired how polite Kameesha's demeanor was. She was growing up so fast.

Any chance Mark got, he would take a picture and send it to his cousin Keith. There were times Keith had made attempts to win Demisha back, but he never asked about Kameesha.

Mark tried to avoid the conflict, but somehow got involved.

Once Mark was content that Kameesha was safe inside the school building, he put the patrol car in drive and drove off.

*

Cookie used her key Demisha gave her to the house. Demisha wasn't answering her phone, plus Cookie knew she was home. The car was parked in front of the house.

Once inside, Cookie noticed the darkness in the home. Demisha had heels and clothes everywhere. "Demisha!" Cookie called out.

No answer.

Cookie went straight to Demisha's bedroom. She saw her curled up in the bed with the TV on. Cookie shook Demisha from her deep sleep. "Wake up! It's time for you to get up."

Demisha pushed Cookie's hand. "Don't you have any respect when somebody trying to sleep?"

"I do, but not when you are partying all night and strange men leaving your house."

"Don't be so concerned. We family," Cookie said.

"And what about Kameesha? What about her? Is she late for school?"

"Kameesha, get your butt to school."

"She not here," Cookie said.

"Let me rest and close the door."

"Get it together, Dee. You need to clean this house and take care of your baby girl."

"Cookie, I'm doing better. Am I in jail? Have I abandoned my daughter?"

"I give you that, Demisha, but being a parent means getting involved in your child's life. When was the last time you walked her to school or helped Kameesha with her homework? She made the honor roll list. She's growing up, and you sleeping your life away."

"Do me a favor," Demisha said.

"What's that?" Cookie said.

Demisha opened her nightstand drawer and handed Cookie a letter. "Drop this in the mailbox for me."

Cookie read the envelope. "This is to a law firm. When did you get in trouble?"

"No trouble. Just trying to pay a bill. I haven't had the chance to get out."

"I wonder why," Cookie said.

Demisha cracked a smile. "I love you, Cookie."

"Time is a gift," Cookie said.

Cookie gave Demisha a hug and left.

CHAPTER 20

Nine years later... August 17, 2020

Darren kept his head down as tears were rolling down his face. The choir was singing "Amazing Grace." Darren was trying to hold back all the emotions he had as his sister was lying in the casket.

After fourteen and a half years of doing hard time, he got released on a Tuesday morning. He had a nice welcome home party. His sister was so vibrant and happy. And then a week later, coming home from a club, leaving with a random dude in his car, she got T-boned on the passenger side.

Demisha was killed on impact.

Darren continued to feel guilty. The weight on his shoulders was heavy.

Darren looked next to him and saw Cookie consoling Kameesha. Cookie had been a true aunt and sister to them.

Darren noticed a familiar face and a stranger enter the Smith Funeral Home as the choir finished the song.

*

Still in his police uniform, Mark and Keith walked into the funeral home. Keith was wearing a gray silk shirt with some black slacks. Keith was older now, with a few gray hairs in his beard.

Keith was scanning the room and saw a huge crowd.

How did Demisha know so many people?

Keith saw Darren look back and turn his head forward. Darren still had that mean look, but was much bigger.

Mark had told him that Darren was with Kameesha, but how would Darren react?

Keith heard the Rev say, "Before we say our last good-byes, her daughter would like to say something."

Kameesha got up and walked over to the small podium.

"Good morning."

The crowd responded back with grace.

Kameesha kept her sunglasses on as she began to speak. "On my mother's nightstand, she kept a picture of her and my uncle Darren. They were so young."

The crowd gave a little laugh.

"I never realized how beautiful my mother was. I never told her that. I'm thankful for never worrying about drugs in the house, police knocking on the door, or CPS doing a welfare check. To my aunt Cookie, for always being there. Thank you, God, for blessing me with a beautiful mom and people who love me."

Kameesha went back to the front and sat next to Cookie.

Cookie gave Kameesha a big hug and a kiss on her cheek.

The Rev. thanked Kameesha for the words about her mother. "Please say your last goodbyes to Kameesha Owens."

Keith and Mark started walking down the aisle.

*

Mark and Keith were standing on the side of the funeral home as people began walking out to their cars. Keith continued to be patient as guests kept walking by.

Cookie, Kameesha, and Darren finally came out.

Keith saw his daughter dressed in an all-black skirt for the first time. He felt overwhelmed by how tall Kameesha was. Her speech really touched him.

Mark had been quiet the whole time. He wished things would have been different between his cousin and Demisha. Maybe she could still be alive.

As Keith made his advance toward the family, Mark followed behind.

"Kameesha," Keith said.

Cookie continued to lead Kameesha to the limo.

Darren stopped Keith in his tracks. "This ain't the time."

"Kameesha, wait—too late for that. I'm her daddy."

Nobody had heard that word for years.

"You been a stranger to her."

"I'm trying to make things right, Darren."

"I'm your father!" Keith yelled.

"You ain't no father."

Darren pushed Keith. Keith pushed him back.

Mark got in between them. Remaining guests from the parking lot began to stare.

"Take your cousin home, Mark."

"Look, let him say what's on his heart," Mark said. "Everybody is hurting."

"Since you trying to be daddy, then what's her favorite food?"

"Cherry Pop-Tarts."

"Her favorite subject in school?"

"I'm not going to play this game."

"Where were you, Keith?"

"You just got out, convict boy!"

"Who you calling boy?"

Darren was trying to put his hands on Keith. Mark pushed Darren back.

"I'm not trying to arrest nobody."

"Look, who tough now?"

"It's not like that, Darren. I'm not that same young kid. I been there for Demisha and Kameesha. You both been absent."

Kameesha was watching everything unfold. She walked over to face the man that her mother always spoke of.

*

Nineteen-year-old Kameesha, standing at five-seven, 170 lbs, with long black hair, kept her eyes on the man that continued to call out her name.

Kameesha saw the resemblance. The same yellow-toned skin and facial features.

As she got closer, her uncle Darren told Kameesha to go back with Cookie at the limo.

Keith continued to say, "Please stay. I'm your father."

Keith was looking at his daughter. She was a spitting image of him. Same dark black hair and matching nose, but hers was a little wide.

"I wasted a lot of years, Kameesha."

Keith noticed the gold bracelet that he bought Demisha on Kameesha's wrist.

"I'm sorry that it had to take your mother to pass away for me to be here. But I'm glad you're wearing the bracelet that I gave her."

Kameesha looked down at the bracelet and was admiring the one thing that her mommy left her to have.

"No more running, Kameesha. Give me a chance."

Kameesha took her sunglasses off. Those same dark brown eyes her father had. There were no tears in Kameesha's eyes. "Those are the magic words I been waiting to hear all my life. You saying you my father. How can I trust your word? You didn't claim me when I was born. Why claim me now?

"I recall when I was eight years old, and my mom asked you

for money to buy me some school clothes. Imagine how kids can remember you wearing the same clothes twice in the same week. You didn't even recognize the fact that I existed. You just walked away."

Darren tried to chime in.

"Uncle, please. I got this."

Darren fell back and walked toward the limo with Cookie.

"Your cousin Mark been there for me more than you have. When I'm ready to engage a conversation with you, be available. It's time for me to walk away from you, Keith."

Kameesha put her shades on and walked away. Her mother would be proud.

Chapter 21

Darren felt good driving around the city with the sun out. He was getting his freedom back. He wished that his sister had kept his Buick, but it had been over fifteen years. He was trying to adjust the driver seat. Darren needed more leg room in his sister's little champ Malibu. As Darren made a right turn, he decided to make a last-minute stop to see about a job.

*

Kameesha was finishing getting out of the shower. Her uncle Darren was moving some boxes out of her mommy's room to the basement. Her uncle wanted to return to the basement, but Kameesha turned it into her braider station.

The times she spent with her mommy were in the basement. Her mother was teaching her how to braid at an early age. She told the story of how her Uncle Darren's girlfriend showed her the skill.

Kameesha continued to think about her mom, which made her sad. Kameesha's thoughts were broken when she heard knocking at the front door.

*

Walking into the Nike shoe factory had Darren thinking he

was in the wrong store. There were displays of so many shoes. It wasn't just a sneaker and hoodie outlet.

Darren stopped a young female salesperson. "Can you get the manager for me?"

The young female said, "Yeah," and disappeared into the back.

A few minutes later, a tall, pasty male came toward Darren. "How can I help you?"

Darren noticed the name tag. "Phil?"

"Yes, I'm Phil."

"Not the young Phil back when Ky owned this store."

"How do you know Ky?"

"I'm Darren."

Phil's eyes got big. "Man, it's been a long time."

Phil gave Darren a firm handshake and a pat on the shoulder. "Man, you got big."

"Working out," Darren said.

"I heard about everything. Ky was really upset."

"Is he here?"

"Not anymore."

"So you're the manager?"

"Yeah, but also the owner."

"What? How?"

"After you got locked up, he didn't care anymore. As time went by, I saved my money, plus a little bank. I bought it from him. The sad thing is he passed away in 2019."

Darren was silent for a moment. "That hurt, man. So much death."

"So what brings you here?" Phil said.

"I need a job, Phil."

"Times are different. A new generation now."

"Shoes are shoes," Darren said.

"We sell Skechers, Hey Dude, and New Balance. Can you keep

up?"

"You know me, Phil. I haven't lost my touch. Pick any shoe and watch me be persuasive. You see those cheerleaders over there? I got some New Balance that are rose sugar and ice wine."

"What? Is that even a color?"

"About regular pink."

"Make the sale, and the job is yours."

"Give me the shoe," Darren said.

Darren put on a smile and headed toward the girls.

*

Darren was making progress as he parked his sister's car. He got out of the car and noticed a green 2015 Dodge Challenger Hellcat leaving from his crib. Hearing that engine roaring made him miss his Buick. He would save some money now that he got his old job back. He had his eye on a '72 Chevelle SS.

Once he watched the Challenger turn the corner, Darren stepped into the house.

*

Kameesha was sitting on the sofa reading Maya Angelou when she heard the door open.

"Hey, Uncle Darren."

"What's up, Butterscotch?"

Kameesha smiled every time she heard her nickname. "Nobody call me that but you."

"That's a niece and uncle thing."

"Who was that leaving?"

"My friend Kevin."

"Your friend, huh?"

"Just friends. We be kickin' it. That's all."

"Next time he around, tell him to stay around when I'm here."

"Are you trying to be my daddy?"

"No," Darren said. "I'm only looking out for you."

"I don't need a daddy. Just be my uncle."

Darren took a deep breath and said, "Okay."

Kameesha got up from the sofa and went into her room and slammed the door.

CHAPTER 22

Darren jumped up from his sleep. He was having a nightmare about his sister.

Darren was trying to adjust his eyes to see the alarm clock. The time was twelve-twenty a.m.

Darren was about to fluff his pillow when he heard some noises. The walls in this house were so thin.

That made Darren jump up and come out of his room.

Darren was banging on Kameesha's door when he heard the headboard stop moving.

Bang! Bang!

"I'm not leaving."

Just then, a tall skinny dude with braids was standing with the door halfway open. "Is there a problem?"

"I appreciate if you don't be disrespectful, because that wasn't the TV."

"Look, who is you? What your name, ol' skool?"

"Uncle Darren."

Kameesha was now at the door with a robe on. "My friend Kevin was just leaving."

"Oh, you Uncle Darren?"

"That's right."

Kevin asked Kameesha to grab his shirt. As Kevin was putting his shirt on, Darren went to the living room and turned on the lights.

"Don't think this is going to be a regular pattern."

"Yeah, okay," Kevin said sarcastically.

Darren wanted to put his hands on Kevin so bad.

Kevin gave Kameesha a kiss on the lips as he was looking at Darren.

Darren was ready to go back to jail.

"Call you later," Kevin said. He walked to the door and left.

"What's your problem, Uncle Darren?"

"I was trying to get some sleep until I heard the headboard." Darren was trying to forget the sound.

"I'm grown. This my house."

"Correction, your grandmother left it to me and your mommy."

"I never had the chance to meet my grandma."

Darren was pointing a finger. "You don't know what..." Darren went silent.

"I'm going to bed, Kameesha. We will talk later," Darren said.

*

When Darren woke up, he noticed Kameesha was already gone. He went into the kitchen to fix some coffee, one of the habits he picked up from prison. As Darren was adding sugar to his cup, he heard the front door open.

"Anyone here!" Cookie shouted.

"In the kitchen," Darren yelled back.

Cookie appeared in her tight correctional uniform. Darren noticed the curves.

"Want some coffee?" Darren asked Cookie.

"I'm good. I was going to call you, but since you're here, how can I get me and Kameesha on the same page? Either she reading a book, in her room, or with that drug dealer Kevin."

"She just dealing with a lot right now, Darren. Just focus on being here full time and tell her you love her. You're home now, so Cookie can get a break."

"Thanks, Cookie, for never abandoning my sister."

"Cookie will always be around. It's time for me to get to work."

"What's the rush?" Darren said. "Must want to walk around all day."

Cookie noticed Darren was hinting at her pants.

"These are my 'I have a man' pants."

Cookie slapped her butt cheeks and left, saying, "See you later."

Darren was leaving the house for work. He saw Mark in regular clothes coming his way. "Man, what you want?"

"There is no need for that tough attitude when you see me. What's on your mind?"

"Heard the Challenger leaving early this morning."

Darren forgot about the new friend. "You know of him?"

"Be around in the neighborhood. His name is Kevin McLittle, A.K.A. Lil Kev. Got a small crew of three that hang around the high school. They call themselves the MAD Boyz."

"What they do?"

"Mayhem All Day. Lifting, drug hustling, robbing."

"Have you arrested him before?"

"Nah, but we will get him soon."

"If you find anything else, let me know," Darren said, then got into the car and headed to work.

"She just dealing with a lot right now, Darren. Just [illegible] here with her and tell her I love her. You're home now so Cookie can get after it."

"Thanks, Cookie, for never abandoning my sister."

"Cookie will always be around. It's time for me to get to you."

"What's the rush?" Darren said. "I don't want to walk around all day."

Cookie noticed Darren was in [illegible] pants.

"These are my [illegible] pants."

Cookie clapped her hurt cheeks and left, saying "See you later."

Darren was leaving the house for work. He saw a dark [illegible] clothes coming his way. "Man, what you want?"

"There is no need for that tough attitude when you see me. What's on your mind?"

"Heard the Challenger leaving early this morning."

Darren forgot about the new friend. "You know of him?"

"He's new in the neighborhood. His name is Kevin [illegible]. [illegible] Got a [illegible] that keep a [illegible] behind [illegible] the MPD [illegible]."

"What they do?"

"Maybe when all [illegible] robbing."

"Have you ever seen him before?"

"Only now [illegible] will get him soon."

"If you find anything else, let me know," Darren said, then got into the car and headed to work.

CHAPTER 23

Over the last few weeks, Darren and Kameesha had passed each other on a daily basis without speaking. Darren would leave for work, and Kameesha had been leaving with Kevin. Darren had his suspicions of Kevin making small drug deals on his block. Kevin's little crew had been hanging around in front of the house. Mark had assured him that all they did was smoke and stand around.

Darren never thought he and Mark would be this close again. At some point, Darren would take accountability and tell Mark he appreciated him stepping in over the years helping out Demisha and Kameesha. For now, Darren would try to communicate with Kameesha about making better choices.

*

Sunday night, Kameesha was coming up from the basement. She had just finished two clients' heads. Darren was sitting in the living room when the two young ladies walked past, heading for the door. Kameesha told them that she would see them in two weeks.

"I have to admit, them girls' hair look nice."

"Yeah. Mommy had a good teacher."

"How come you never talk about her?"

"Who? Your mom?"

"No. Kim."

Darren hadn't heard that name in years. "She was around when you was little. We had some good times."

"Did you love her?"

"Of course I did."

"So what happened?"

"Too much time has passed. I took her for granted. I was being selfish. I was only considering my feelings."

Kameesha could see the smile on her uncle's face. "Do you miss her?"

"I do sometimes."

"Why you haven't tried to reach out?"

"When the time is right, I will."

"When is the right time?"

Trying to change the subject, Darren wanted to say something to Kameesha. "I like the little gift that you gave me, your graduation picture, and put it on the nightstand next to your mom. I'm sorry for not being there. But I have to ask, what's up with this Kevin dude? He just a friend?"

"Yeah, he is, unc."

"Just be careful. He trouble."

"I will, unc."

Darren got up and went to give Kameesha a hug. "You know I love you, right?"

"I know," Kameesha said and walked to her room and closed the door.

*

The next day, Lil Kevin was sitting on Kameesha's bed counting some money while Kameesha was in the basement. Each time he counted, the money was off. He was missing two thousand dollars. Most of the time, Kevin would count the profits at his stash spot. He was thinking about putting a safe in Kameesha's room. This is why he could never trust nobody in this business. Somebody always got sticky fingers and break the rules. Never steal from Kevin.

Kevin got off the bed and lifted the mattress up. Nothing there. He checked under the bed. He went to the closet and checked the top shelf. Moved a few shoe boxes around. Being tall, he saw a gray metal box. He grabbed the gray box and sat it on the bed. He unlatched the box and saw hundred-dollar bills. There were a few pictures of Kameesha and some lady he never saw. Kameesha did mention her momma passing away. It could be her.

But Kevin was upset about the cash.

He took all the money out and counted it. There was seventeen hundred. "This trick is spending my money, acting like she don't have any."

Kevin flung the door open and headed for the basement.

*

Kameesha was doing some twists on Cookie's hair. It was the first time Cookie sat down in the chair that belonged to Demisha.

"I feel special right now," Cookie said. "The last person to do my hair was your momma."

"Well, I'm glad you trust me, Auntie Cookie," Kameesha said, laughing.

As they continued to talk, Kameesha saw Kevin come downstairs with rage.

"What's wrong?" Kameesha asked.

Kevin didn't say a word. He slapped Kameesha.

"You stealing from me."

Cookie was in shock and went to grab Kevin. "Punk, don't be

putting your hands on my niece."

Cookie was no match for Kevin's tall frame. He grabbed Cookie and shoved her down.

Kameesha was dazed by the slap, but managed to focus and ran up the stairs. Kevin was fast on her heels. As the commotion headed upstairs, Cookie grabbed her cellphone and called Darren.

Darren picked up on the first ring. "Why you calling? I thought you was getting your hair done."

"Forget that! Get here now!"

"What's wrong?"

Darren already had his foot on the gas pedal.

"That boy just shoved me down and slapped Kameesha."

Darren ended the call with Cookie and called Mark.

Mark was at the station when his phone rang. "This is Mark."

"I need your help. Mark, this is Darren."

"What's the problem?"

"Just get to my house ASAP."

Darren pressed end on the phone.

CHAPTER 24

Kameesha was hysterical as she ran into the bathroom and closed the door. It had a little latch on it. She could already hear Kevin screaming.

"You can't hide from me." Kevin's voice became closer. He grabbed the knob and was trying to open it, banging on the door. "Why you stealing from me? I kill people for that."

Kameesha was crying. "I don't have to steal from you. I didn't do it, Kevin."

Kevin kicked the door. On the fourth kick, the door burst open.

Kevin now had one hand on Kameesha's throat. He was shaking her like a rag doll. With his free hand, Kevin made a fist and cocked his hand all the way back, then brought it forward with all his strength.

Kameesha's lip cracked open and bled.

Cookie screamed, "Help!"

*

Darren was driving up the block like he was a NASCAR driver. He didn't even turn the car off. He put it in park and jumped out.

He ran toward the door and saw Cookie. Cookie just pointed down the hallway where all the arguing was happening.

Darren rushed to the back and saw Kevin's full body frame over Kameesha.

Darren jumped Kevin from behind and was able to get him in a chokehold position. Kevin was trying to break the grip, but Darren was squeezing tight.

Kevin was trying to push backward. Darren had his legs planted well.

Cookie was yelling, "Kill him!"

Darren told Cookie to grab the bat behind the couch. She went and found the aluminum bat, and as she was returning to the bathroom, Darren was dragging Kevin out of the bathroom.

Cookie told Darren to turn him around. Once Darren did, Cookie tried to hit Kevin. She hit his feet and kneecaps. Cookie wanted to bust him in the head, but was afraid she might hit Darren.

"This is for my niece," Cookie said, and hit Kevin in the nuts.

Kevin let out a scream.

Darren unleashed his arms from Kevin's neck.

Kevin was holding his nuts.

Darren grabbed the bat from Cookie and said, "My turn."

Darren took the bat and went to work.

*

Mark had the police siren on as he was pulling up to the Owens house. Mark took his gun out of his holster and proceeded into the house.

With his gun drawn, Mark entered the house and saw Darren with the bat.

Darren was yelling, "Don't you ever put your funky hands on my niece."

Mark gave Darren a command. "Drop the bat."

"Not until he's dead."

"I don't want to shoot you. I need you to put the bat down."

Darren wasn't in the mood to hear nobody. Kevin took Darren to a dark space where he didn't want to go.

"If you kill him, you go back to jail."

"So what?"

"What about Kameesha?"

Darren stopped midair.

"Do it for Kameesha," Mark said. "Put the bat down."

Mark could hear other police sirens coming.

"Toss the bat, Darren."

Kevin's body was limp.

Cookie was now holding Kameesha in the hallway.

"Is he still breathing?" Cookie asked.

Mark's only concern was to get Darren away from Kevin.

Mark told Darren to turn around. Mark took his cuffs out and walked to Darren.

Mark was leading Darren to his patrol car as the other Gary police cars showed up.

Mark told Darren that he had his back.

*

Seven months later...

As Darren was sitting in courtroom two with the orange jumpsuit on, it was déjà vu all over again. How could he end up with the same judge? Don't they get old and retire?

Judge Wilson was now bald and wrinkled. His mustache was pure white. The judge put on his glasses and looked at Darren. "It seems after fifteen years you continue to be in my courtroom."

Darren continued to look at the judge as his public defender began speaking. "Your Honor, my client was only trying to defend his family."

The prosecutor jumped in. "The defendant, Your Honor, beat the man with a bat."

"Is he alive?" the judge asked.

"Barely, Your Honor."

"How do you want to proceed, Ms. Ashley?" the judge asked.

"Assault one and attempted murder."

Darren was shaking his head. He told the public defender he wanted to speak.

His public defender chimed in. "Your Honor, my client would like to say something, if it pleases the court."

"Go ahead, Mr. Owens."

"Thank you, Judge Wilson. After fifteen years, I didn't want to return to your courtroom. I was doing good for myself. Working, saving money, and trying to raise my niece. I lost my mother due to a controlling boyfriend, a sister that died from a car crash, and I almost lost my niece due to a drug dealer. I would rather be in jail knowing that my niece is alive. I'm willing to accept my part, Your Honor."

The judge told both sides he would review the matter and set a continuance for thirty days.

*

The next day, on a Saturday afternoon, Darren was sitting in the dayroom when the officer came into the WB pod and called out, "Owens."

Darren approached the C.O. and told him he was Owens. The male C.O. told him he had a visit.

Darren followed the C.O. up some stairs. After the officer hit the keypad, the door buzzed open. He told Darren to enter and walk up the stairs.

Darren made his way up the stairs and saw all the seats and big window panels. He looked into each one until he saw Mark.

Darren sat down and picked up the phone.

"What you doing here? You're not on my list."

"I'm police, remember?"

"I forget sometimes."

"I just wanted to tell you that I talked with the prosecutor and gave my statement to the events that happened."

"What you say?" Darren said.

"The truth. When I entered the house, you was protecting two female victims that was in fear of their lives. You had no choice but to use the bat. Plus, we sent them pictures of Kameesha's face from the hospital."

Darren didn't want to see them.

"What does that mean for me?"

"Judge Wilson is contemplating on dropping the charges and time served."

"Thank you, man," Darren said.

"Continue to have faith. I told you, I got you."

"You been all right, Mark. I can respect you, Uncle Mark."

"That means a lot," Mark said. "Somebody else wanted to see you."

Mark got up and walked away.

Kameesha came and sat down.

Darren was smiling at his niece. Kameesha had a pink patch over her right eye and a little scar on her lip where Kevin had hit her.

"So what the doctor say about your eye?"

"It might be fractured, but I go see the eye specialist next week."

"How you holding up, unc?"

"This is small potatoes. I'm surviving."

"I just wanted to say I'm sorry for acting out. When you went to prison, I didn't have a male figure in my life. I didn't know how a male supposed to treat me. If any boy gave me attention or brought me gifts, I thought that was love. So when Kevin came around, he always said that I had natural beauty, never needed makeup. He was the one for me."

Darren was wiping his eyes. "I'm sorry for not being there. That's on me. But I'm here now. Kevin was no man. He was a liability. He would lie in your face and have the ability to take advantage of you. No woman should be treated that way."

"One question," Darren said.

"What's that?" Kameesha said.

"Not that it matters. Did you take his money?"

"No, unc. Mommy left me a life insurance policy."

"Oh, really? I didn't know."

"It's cool. I got you."

"I will always love you, Butterscotch."

"Thank you, Uncle Darren."

"Before I go, I got one more thing to say."

"What's that?" Darren said.

"You know what tomorrow is?"

Darren was thinking. "No clue."

"Happy Father's Day," Kameesha said.

Kameesha put her hand on the window panel. Darren matched his hand with hers.

ACKNOWLEDGEMENTS

To my sister who gave birth to my precious niece, thank you for giving her a special name.

To my big bro Solo, who pushed me to write.

To my guy Pope for the original artwork.

To Kameesha, may you live your life however you see fit.

Your Uncle, Ronnie R.E.D.D. Rice loves you.

ABOUT THE AUTHOR

Ronnie Redd Rice is serving a life sentence at Wabash Valley Correctional Facility. In his small cell, Rice continues to feed what he loves to do—writing. He uses his work to reexamine life in prison. REALIZE EVERYTHING DON'T DEPRECIATE is his motivation.

Every story needs hope.

www.ingramcontent.com/pod-product-compliance
Lightning Source LLC
LaVergne TN
LVHW030922080826
845145LV00013B/3017